"Men were as proud of
a good team of horses
as people are of a shiny,
new car today."

– Earl Vandewater, 2011

K.K.
Treasure the journey...
Ruschie Vandewater Engle
– 2012 –

To: K.K.
Enjoy!
Lisa Sprague

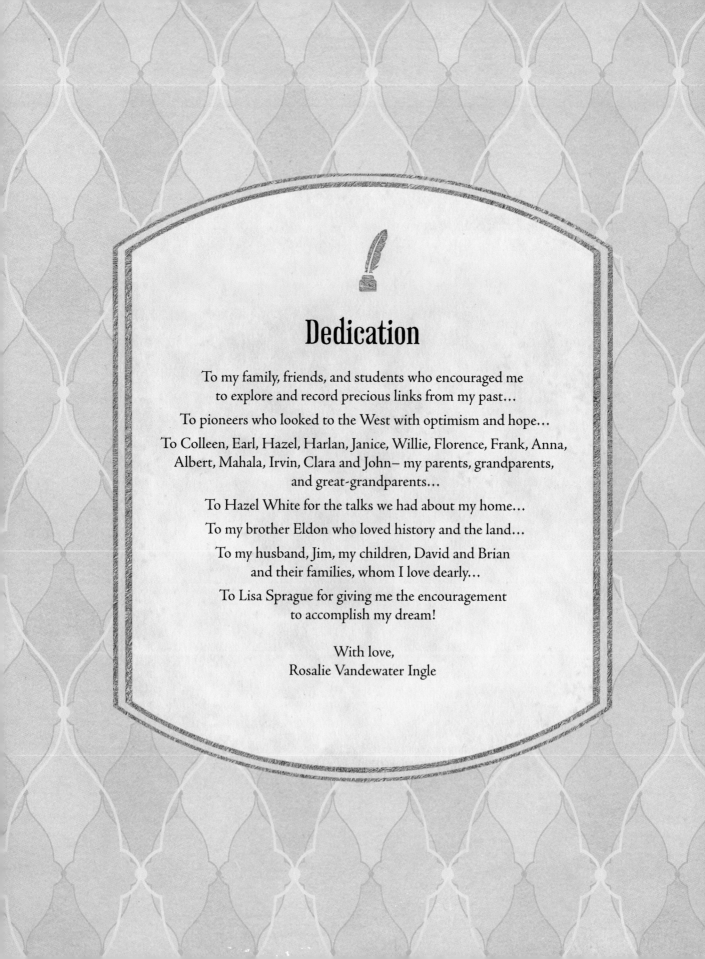

Dedication

To my family, friends, and students who encouraged me
to explore and record precious links from my past…

To pioneers who looked to the West with optimism and hope…

To Colleen, Earl, Hazel, Harlan, Janice, Willie, Florence, Frank, Anna,
Albert, Mahala, Irvin, Clara and John– my parents, grandparents,
and great-grandparents…

To Hazel White for the talks we had about my home…

To my brother Eldon who loved history and the land…

To my husband, Jim, my children, David and Brian
and their families, whom I love dearly…

To Lisa Sprague for giving me the encouragement
to accomplish my dream!

With love,
Rosalie Vandewater Ingle

The Stage is Coming!

HALLIE'S STAGE STOP JOURNEY

HALLIE

Written by ROSALIE VANDEWATER INGLE

Illustrations by LISA CAROL SPRAGUE

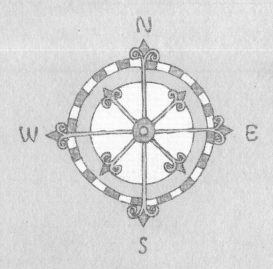

I REMEMBER THE DAY I LEFT ILLINOIS IN 1870 TO TRAVEL WEST with my mama, papa, and brother, Will. Papa said a new life awaited us in Iowa. Our promised home had become a popular stage stop during the Western Expansion. The Mormon Trail, used by followers of the Mormon faith to cross Iowa beginning in 1846, ran within yards of our home. It still led many travelers on hired stagecoaches, in covered and open wagons, and on horseback looking for rest, food, and shelter. "People will always be searching for a better life," Papa said. Weary after days of riding, men, women, and children found refuge in our large, rambling house. Stagecoach lines continued to flourish in Iowa into the 1870s, when railways for steam engines were being established. Many of the coaches and wagons we saw came from the Mount Pisgah area and followed the worn trail near Buffalo Wallow making their way toward Council Bluffs. Papa said that we would continue business at our stage stop even after the railroad was up and running in the nearby towns. We opened our home to these travelers, fed them and offered them our beds, and in return they gave us stories of adventure and the latest news from the East. For me, life on the prairie leading people to the West was exciting, and I willingly welcomed the journey ahead.

My Journey West, 1870   15 days, 300 miles

Our Journey Begins April 1870

I carefully wrapped the colorful quilt my aunt pieced for me and enclosed a small carved wooden doll, dressed in blue gingham, made by my grandpa. I filled a handkerchief with hollyhock seeds from Grandma's garden and tied it tightly so I could sow them in Iowa to remind me of our dear home in Illinois. I placed these items into a small trunk for Papa to put under the seat of the open wagon. As I wiped my tears, our mules John and Toby led our wagon west.

I was just 11 and my brother Will was 13 when Papa bought the land in Iowa with the existing stage stop. Our new home, designed and built to be operated as a hotel in a bustling city, stood stately in the middle of the Iowa prairie in Adair County. The home in Orient Township became a resting stop for travelers migrating along the Mormon Trail. My papa was excited but short on words, so when he spoke, we listened. "We have a chance to own a piece of land and run a business. It will be hard, but we must work together," Papa said. He was a serious man. His large, calloused hands came from years of hard work tending the soil as a farmer. He stood tall, nearly six feet in height. Mama did not say much that day. She sat quietly in our wagon and carefully smoothed the apron that covered her hand-stitched cotton print dress. A small locket hung just below the high collar of the dress bodice, and a comb loosely held back her brown hair. Tan cotton stockings covered her legs, and practical leather shoes were securely laced on her feet. A sunbonnet shielded her head, hiding the tears from us. I sensed she did not want to leave friends and family, but Papa assured us we would have a good life.

On a cool day in April we followed two other wagons filled with families seeking new opportunities on the prairie, too. I felt excited, yet uneasy about the adventure ahead. Wooden crates carried clothes and household supplies needed for the move, and a large steamer trunk held Mama's cherished family heirlooms. Papa secured all of our

belongings with rope, and a coop full of chickens hung on the back of the wagon. Papa said that not everything could fit into the small open farm wagon, so we left many cherished possessions behind. Mama and Papa sat in front, steering the mules. Will and I sat side by side, between cargo, as we began our journey of 20 days of travel. Going 15 miles per day to make the 300 mile trek, we traveled dirt roads, mud roads, through streams, and beside twisting rivers. Our route followed east to west across the middle of Iowa until we headed south to our home. We only rested at stage stops along the way when money allowed and bad weather prevailed.

"Hold on to your bonnet, Hallie," Mama called out. "Our new home is just ahead." Suddenly Papa let out a big whoop and shouted, "We're here!" We rounded the last curve just ahead of our final stage stop. A large, two-story white house surrounded by tall waving prairie grass welcomed us home.

skeleton key

Summer on the Prairie

During the first days of summer I often waited under the drooping limbs of the willow tree that stood in front of our house. I patiently listened for the familiar sound of horses' hooves which meant that new travelers would soon arrive.

Summer weather in Iowa was hot and humid, so the willow provided not only a cool place to rest, but a quiet place to reflect. "Will I travel to distant cities in the West? What do the cities look like?" I thought. "What clothes do people wear as they walk down city streets?" I leaned back against the trunk of the tree and looked up at the maze

of limbs, branches, and leaves. I imagined them as the winding paths and roads running in all directions that carried people out West. I remembered the muddy roads, swollen rivers, and the many challenges we faced and wondered if others experienced the same. I knew many dreamed of California or Oregon and the promise for a new life. Papa often chuckled, "Some men think gold is hanging off them mountains in California, and they'll be rich." Mama would say in a soft voice, "I think some families want their own piece of land and perhaps raise some chickens." Papa told us many people faced disappointment and hard times after making their way to the West. I did not like to think about those sad stories. The West to me sounded very exciting.

Our Stage Stop, a Welcoming Sight

I breathed in deeply the sweet smell of honeysuckle. Giant cottonwood trees and maple trees towered above the lane leading to the pastures. Grapevines tumbled around posts in the garden behind the house. As I carried my small wooden doll around, I explored and inspected Grandma's hollyhock seeds growing by the pump. Life on the prairie was hard, and there was much work to be done. Every morning I collected eggs, fed the geese, and helped bring the cows in from the fields for milking. However, there were many wonderful things, too, such as stealing away moments by myself.

I ran toward the wide front porch, jumped up the two small stairs, and stood between the pillars where I looked in all directions at the land. I saw the trail leading to the house, the fields of crops, and in the evening I watched the sun setting in the west. I waited for visitors by sitting on the stoop reading a book or gazed at the latest fashion in an old *Godey's Magazine and Lady's Book*, given as a gift from a befriended traveler. To me the porch was a great place to spend idle hours before a coach arrived. Sometimes I pretended it was my stage and I, an actress of the prairie. Like a fairy floating across a magical platform, I wrapped my special quilt around my shoulders and bowed gracefully

to an imaginary audience. The quilt fell loosely from my shoulders, lightly touching the wooden planks. I recalled the day my aunt gave me the flower garden quilt. "Wrap this around you to remember me. I stitched this quilt with my own hands just for you," she proudly said. As I glided toward the porch's edge, I twirled the quilt in the air and bowed again only to the sight of blowing prairie grass and rolling tumbleweeds.

Suddenly, the distant sound of horses' hooves jolted me from my pretend play. I knew this sound well because it was a part of my life now.

A stagecoach the size of my thumb was getting closer, growing larger as it rumbled up our dirt road. I continued to watch as it rounded the last bend, heading toward the row of elm trees south of my house. Dust billowed from beneath the wooden wheels, and sagebrush tumbled to the side of the road. The stagecoach headed for my house, my family's business. Play would wait. Work was ahead.

I left the quilt on a nearby bench and jumped down the front steps. I started to run along the dirt path by the side of the house. My brown pigtails flopped against my freckled face. My cotton print dress, layered by an apron tied at the waist, slowed me down a bit as it swayed from side to side. Dust billowed around my bare feet, feeling warm and loose between my toes. The hot wind hit my face, and I longed for a quick drink of water from the well pump behind the house before the coach arrived.

"The stage is coming!" "The stage is coming!" I shouted. I raced to the back of the house to find my parents. I knew the passengers inside the coach eagerly awaited a rest from their trip. The distance of 15 miles often separated stops, and many rode for days before that, only stopping when fresh horses replaced the tired ones or to spend the night at a stage stop. The riders desperately longed for food, conversation, and rest before they continued west.

"The Stage is coming! The Stage is coming!" I hollered again.

I looked toward the large sprawling house and expected its grandeur to be a surprising sight to our company. The white paint gave the two-story house a graceful presence as the stagecoaches approached from the south. A wide porch with spiral columns covered a good portion of the front. Ivy twined around a separate small courting porch. Benches on both sides supplied a captivating place to think or a spot for quiet conversation. Carved wooden scrolls behind the seats gave a whimsical detail to the otherwise functional house. Another large porch framed the back of the house and was enclosed for more practical, everyday duties.

A House with a Purpose

We used the back porch during all seasons. In the winter Papa placed sheeting over the screen to protect the space from the harsh winter. "Coming through with a bucket of milk," Papa said. At that cue Mama and I took the milk and waited until the cream rose to the top. Then we scooped the cream off with a wooden paddle or sometimes with just our hands. Narrow steps led to a dirt floor basement where root vegetables and green beans preserved in brine sat on lined, flat wooden shelves, stored for the winter. A lantern hung on the inside of the porch door for Papa to use when he went to the barn at night to check on the animals. This area also was a place to recover from a day's work for our family and the farm hands. Papa often said, "Take your boots off and come in and cool off." In the summer months Papa and Will rested there after the early morning hours of work just before lunch.

Mama and I washed clothes in this *porch room*. We gave dirty clothes a good scrubbing on a washboard which leaned against the side of a wooden tub. Mama made lye soap in a black kettle with water heated on the wood stove.

The Kitchen

The kitchen became the central attraction of our home. Mama scurried around checking coals and added twigs to increase heat from the large wood cooking stove in the corner of the kitchen. Wood for the stove came from a nearby government-owned forest along the 102 River. Papa made frequent trips to cut wood and loaded it in the wagon. The wood proved vital because the cooking stove was not only a necessity for cooking but also for heating the home during the long winter months.

tea kettle

Butler's Pantry

Adjoining the kitchen was a small butler's pantry with wooden shelves built to the ceiling to store food. Many times Mama anxiously said, "Hallie, get me some green beans from the stone jar on the shelf." I knew that Mama needed them quickly to finish up a meal. She patiently waited in the hot kitchen, wearing an apron and wiping the sweat from her forehead, until I handed them to her. The pantry also contained shelves for dishes, linen, and cutlery. In the corner a small hand pump brought water from a cistern beside the house. Rainwater drained off the roof and filled the cistern. We did not drink this water, but used it for washing hands and cooking. A slop bucket sat in the corner of the pantry to hold scraps of food and other remnants from meal preparation. We passed food and dishes from the pantry to the dining area through a small opening in the wall. I liked to peek through the opening to see our special guests.

The Dining Room

The long pine table in the dining room held up to fifteen people. A wood stove stood in the corner for much needed warmth in winter. It sat on the opposite side of the wall from the kitchen's cooking stove. Chimney pipes ran from each stove to a hole in the wall which carried smoke out through the chimney on the roof. At night homemade talo candles and kerosene lamps lit this area, as well as the upstairs. After the end of the day's chores and duties, Mama and I often read or sewed in this dim light.

Here Comes Company!

The steady sound of hooves on the packed dirt and the sight of flaring horses' nostrils captured my attention. Sweat dripped from under the horses' harness. *Clop, clop, clop.* I glanced up at the new stage. These travelers provided a welcome break from the hard work on the prairie. I grew excited each time a new stage, wagon or horse pulled up to the stage stop. I wondered where they came from and was curious about where they were going. I enjoyed the news each visitor told of the East and reveled in the stories of optimism they told about the West. Perhaps a girl my age rode on the stagecoach thinking the same thing. Was she wondering about her new home? Was she excited about moving further west? What will her new life be like? Each person told their story, and I listened to each one eagerly. Would I tell stories to others about my travels someday I secretly wondered?

I ran to the water pump just in time to see our guests arrive. *Pump, pump, pump.* The water splashed out. I put my mouth close to the spout and took a long slurp of water. It tasted cold and refreshing. One drink would do until later. I grabbed a wooden bucket hanging on a nearby fence and started pumping hard. *Pump, pump, pump.* I needed to fill the bucket quickly. With the pail nearly full, I turned to run toward the stage. My cotton dress wrapped around my ankles, and for a brief moment I felt the bucket slip out of my hands. The wire handle pinched me, but I grasped it tighter. Water splashed on my feet and hit the ground, making *splish splash* dots in the soft dirt, but I managed to hold on. With the water bucket in my hand, I caught up with Mama, Papa, and the farm hand at the edge of the dirt path. The stagecoach driver pulled on the reins to signal the horses to stop. "*Whoa, horses, whoa. Whoa!*" With a strong jerk of the reins, the horses and stagecoach came to a complete stop.

The passengers departed the stage slowly. I could tell they were sore and tired from the long ride on wooden benches inside the coach. Each one looked dusty and

windblown. Their cracked, parched lips showed days in the sun. As they climbed down the wooden steps of the stagecoach, I listened to their chatter. I sensed their eagerness to get out of the coach as I ran closer to get a look at the riders on this particular stage run.

"Hallie, hurry over here and help the ladies with their bags," Papa commanded. "Get along girl, the folks are tired and need rest."

I glanced at the sweaty group as they continued to depart the stage. Two ladies in bustle skirts and bonnets made their way gingerly down the steps. I watched as they lifted their skirts just above their ankles to maneuver the coach stairs, revealing high

laced shoes. "Oh, how I wish I had a pair of shoes like those instead of my worn, brown leather boots," I thought wistfully. Veils attached to their bonnets protected their faces from the dust during the journey. A young girl in a plain cotton dress also wore a bonnet and followed carefully behind. Each lady carried a tapestry bag. I wondered if it held the fancy store-bought dresses with buttons up the back that I read about in my magazines. Two men and a boy came down the steps last, holding their leather satchels. Suspenders held up their dust-covered, wrinkled pants. Sometimes up to eighteen passengers crowded onto a stage, up to nine sitting on three seats inside the coach and as many as nine on top. This stage, however, held a small group of only seven.

"Young lady, this is a mighty fine place you have here," one gentleman remarked. "Sure are lucky to have a stop like this. Most are not this fancy. Where's the pump? My throat is parched."

Will helped the coach driver hand down small bags from the top. Will wore cuffed denim overalls and leather work boots. His tasseled hair hung low on his forehead. He chewed on a piece of straw and politely nodded to everyone as he fetched the bags.

In a rough, gravelly voice, the driver bellowed, "Throwing down only the necessary bags. Large baggage remains onboard." Rawhide chaps covered his pants and a kerchief hung at his neck. During the stage ride the handkerchief was pulled up to keep dust from his nostrils. A wide-brim hat nearly covered his leathery, dusty face. He stepped down, stretched his arms high in the air, and walked to the back of the stagecoach to check on the luggage stowed at the rear. Baggage was covered with a tanned hide flap held down with straps. "Need to be ready to depart early in the morning," he said. "These bags stay here." I glanced to see the large steamer trunks still on top of the coach. "I would love to see the dresses inside those trunks," I thought again to myself.

The Travelers' Belongings

Ladies usually carried a small cloth garment bag that stored overnight necessities. Men carried leather satchels. I liked to listen to Papa as he explained their probable contents. "Men carry razors and shaving mugs. Some brought an extra bandana and a change of clothes. You do not need much out here on the prairie. Ladies, well you know what they carry in their bags. Many save a special dress for arrival at their destination. Don't know why they fuss about how they look out here," Papa quipped. Along with the trunks, larger parcels and government mail remained on the stagecoach. I wondered about the documents in the mail pouches. A sense of mystery came with each new stage. I liked being a part of the Western Expansion.

The Most Precious Cargo... The Horses

mass-produced horseshoes

Papa led the horses to a nearby well to drink. Will then cooled them down, took them to the barn, and fed them oats and corn in a wooden trough. It was funny when he threw them whole ears of corn. The horses rolled them over and over to get them ready to eat. A large wooden barn stood east of the house and served an important purpose at the stage stop. It was designed to hold many horses in stalls and had a separate side for milking cows. One double door was at the southeast corner. Above the main floor was a hayloft. A wide door in the loft enabled hay to be put in the barn or thrown down when needed. Will tossed the hay from the loft with a pitchfork to make a layered bed where the horses slept. Chickens noisily roamed throughout the barn. Will and I wandered in the hayloft when there were no chores to do. Through the hayloft door we saw for miles over fields and timber. In the morning Will gently rubbed the horses with small curry combs and brushed them before they were harnessed up as a team to the stagecoach. Will and Papa were proud of the horses when they left our stop. Another day's trek on the prairie began again for our guests.

Room and Rest for the Weary, and Us Too

After travelers used the "privy" or outhouse, Mama called to me, "Show the ladies up the to the front porch."

"Step this way, ladies," I said as they made their way up the wooden steps to the porch. "Step carefully, a loose plank or two might give way if you don't step right. This porch is for sitting in the evening or for cooling off in the afternoon. It catches a nice breeze from the south. Just pull up a chair and make yourself comfortable." I had rehearsed that speech many times, but my favorite part was soon to come. "If you happen to be a courtin' or a newlywed or such, the porch on the side will suit you just fine."

From the porch I led them through a screen door into the large dining room. A long pine table held dishes set for the evening meal. Bay windows to the south gave a panoramic view of the stage path and the barn to the east. During the summer the windows let in refreshing breezes that drifted

21

through the rooms, a welcome respite from the summer heat. Mama offered drinking water poured from a white ironstone pitcher. With their thirst quenched, I led each guest up the narrow wooden stairs to one of the three bedrooms on the second floor. Each spacious room boasted a large closet built with wide shelves to store baggage and heavy trunks. Simple, efficient rooms with quilt covered beds, a wash stand with a pitcher filled with water for freshening up, and a small chamber pot beside each bed, provided the necessities. Stark walls framed each room with splashes of color displayed by the patchwork bed quilt and a hand painted crock pitcher. A multi-colored hooked rug lay across the wood plank floor and gave a cheery spirit to each room. This hooked rug was useful for warmth in the winter, too, when feet hit the icy cold floor. An attic above the kitchen gave extra room for storage.

Despite the lack of frills and elaborate fabrics and amenities found in bedrooms back East, I liked these rooms. From the windows in each room I saw the vast prairie in all directions. In the spring I watched Papa plant fields of corn, wheat, oats, and barley. I watched the spring rains fall on newly planted fields. On those days, with the rain beating against the stage stop, I felt safe and content. A good book sometimes kept my attention, or Mama frequently gave me a tatting project or asked for help with piecing a quilt. Mama liked to make doilies that we placed around the rooms on tables and dressers. She used needle and thread to repair ripped clothing and darning needles to mend stockings. I helped with those sewing projects, too. Rainy days seemed less physically demanding. With chores done, Will and I often ran outside to splash through the puddles of water standing in the ditches. The rain felt cool and soothing on my bare feet. I found peace on the prairie.

My family and I slept together in a downstairs bedroom when a stage arrived full of people or when boarders stayed several months. The men travelers rested on beds arranged in rows or on the floor in the large room upstairs. Women and children took the other two rooms which held regular beds and trundle beds. The farmhand bunked in any open room available.

Hallie's Secret Stairway

Below the staircase was a secret hiding place just large enough for me to fit in. A metal latch held the door shut, and sometimes I slowly lifted the latch so no one could hear me. Inside my special space was our family trunk containing our most valuable possessions from back East. I liked to peek inside at the treasures. A pieced quilt lay on the bottom and protected a flow blue teacup and saucer that came from Grandma's cabinet in Illinois. Mama's wedding dress remained folded on the side. Our family Bible rested prominently on top.

Sometimes at night I heard mice scurrying around the rooms and in the walls. Bedsprings creaked. Outside, owls hooted from their perch in the trees. Coyotes and wolves howled in the distance. I grabbed my special quilt and held it tight around me. Those noises I began to recognize and not fear.

Meal Time

"Hallie, can you come help me with supper?" Mama hollered from downstairs. Mama always wore an apron over her print dress. She had one for "kitchen" wear and a special apron when neighbors stopped by or when the school marm visited. When she worked in the garden, she liked an apron with pockets to hold vegetables. Sometimes Mama just folded the bottom of her apron up around whatever she was carrying so it would hold more. It seemed like Mama was always working; yet, she took time to read us letters from our family back East, or to pen a letter back.

As I approached the kitchen I saw Mama putting a loaf of bread into the oven. I smelled roasted chicken, potatoes, and carrots. Some days Mama served vegetable stew. Travelers always welcomed Mama's strong coffee. We heard that some stops only offered beans, but not at Mama's stop. She took pride in her meals. I filled pitchers of water from the nearby outside pump and readied the glasses for our meal. Mama carried food to the large dining room table. A small parlor adjoined the dining room. Folding doors opened to make it a special room. We used it only when neighbors dropped by to visit or when the young round-faced school marm, Miss Kate, stayed over during bad weather.

Papa said we needed to learn the necessary things of education, so we walked about a mile to the school house. During bad weather Papa took us in a buggy pulled by our horse, Birdie. In the fall and winter this building served as a gathering place for neighbors where singing was taught. Mama made sure that I learned to sing, and I think she enjoyed the lessons, too. It was a fun time with everyone joining in on the songs.

Mama's Coffee Secret

Roast coffee beans quickly.
When almost done roasting, stir a whole egg
into the coffee beans and grind up, shell and all.
Add a bit of sweet butter and mix all together.
Put the powder in the coffee pot in the
proportions of an ounce to a pint of water.
Pour additional boiling water into the pot.

*Mama thought the eggshells and butter
made the coffee richer to serve to her guests.*

*heirloom
beets*

bean grinder

spring peas

Our Family, Growing Through the Seasons

A large garden provided fresh vegetables in the summer, and Mama dried fruits and pickled vegetables for use in the winter months. This process took many hours, and in the hot humid summer of Iowa, it proved to be an exhausting job. Mama worked hard, knowing that the canned products meant meals in the winter months. Food properly preserved kept for several years. Will and I carried full stone crocks of garden goods to the storm cellar, which was a large cave with a mound of dirt on top. It doubled as a storage area for the labors of summer work and a place to keep garden crops through winter. The coolness helped to safely maintain the freshness of eggs and root crops for a short while. Neighbors to our south kept food from perishing by storing it in their water well instead of a cellar. We sometimes stood on top of the grassy, mounded root cellar. In case of a tornado, which was common on the prairie, the cellar doubled as a safe place to ride out the storm.

cochin hen

Chickens, ducks, wild game, pork and beef served as meat sources for our family's stage stop meals. Poultry feathers filled mattresses and pillows.

welsummer rooster

Nothing wasted under mother's frugal watch. If certain crops didn't produce enough, nearby farmers offered items for trade. Mama was known for her garden vegetables and neighbors contributed many hens for her hard labor.

Spring Awakening

On spring days after tending the garden with Mama, I helped to ready the house for the next group of travelers. Once or twice a week wash hung from the clothes line, a piece of heavy wire nailed between two wooden posts. Doing the laundry took most of the day, so I made many trips to the line. The garments smelled fresh when I placed them close to my nose. Wintertime was different. With fewer travelers stopping by, clothes drooped from rope lines strung across the dining room. The wet fabrics and the coldness of winter reminded me that spring would soon arrive. I longed for new travelers, new stories, and the gentle scent of honeysuckle and wild roses. In spring new leaves budded on the elm trees, and the weeping willow in front of the house turned a luscious shade of green.

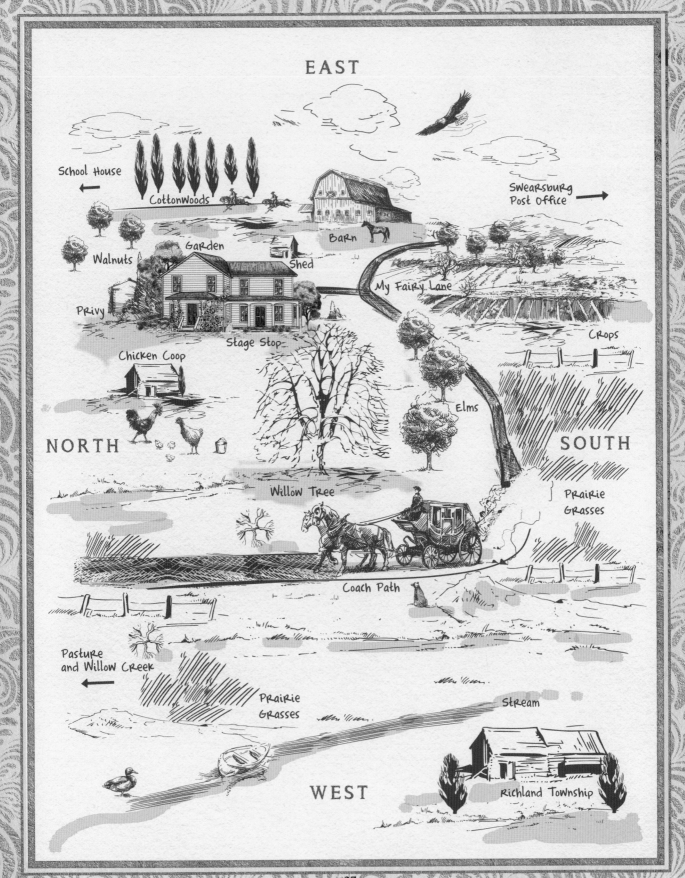

EAST

School House

CottonWoods

Walnuts

Garden

Shed

Barn

My Fairy Lane

Swearsburg
Post Office

Crops

Privy

Stage Stop

Chicken Coop

NORTH

Willow Tree

Elms

SOUTH

Prairie
Grasses

Coach Path

Pasture
and Willow Creek

Prairie
Grasses

Stream

WEST

Richland Township

27

Summer Follies

In the summer the fields became a maze of wistful colors of yellows, browns, and greens. I often took off my shoes and ran barefoot up the dirt lanes beside the fields. In those moments I felt free. The field to the north became our baseball field. My brother and I used sticks and a makeshift ball made of twine, or sometimes a hedge apple, for games with neighboring friends, who walked across fields to join the fun. Long dirt paths allowed room to ride or race ponies. We rode past Dillow Hill, the school house to the south, and looked for muskrats in a nearby creek. Sometimes we just sat at Willow Creek and fished.

Autumn on the Prairie

I loved this time of year. Gold and rust-colored leaves fell, and there was a crisp chill to the air as Papa harvested the last of the crops for fodder, which was food for the horses and cows. Prairie chickens made their nests, readying for the long winter ahead. We prepared for the threat of prairie fires after the grass turned brown and dry. Tumbleweeds carried fire from abandoned campsites and threatened crops and homes. Papa and the hired hand prevented these fires from reaching the stage stop by plowing the ground a good distance around the buildings. The tilled soil kept the fires from spreading.

A Long Cold Winter

Winter arrived with a blustery, freezing spell. The house became very cold, and we slept on cots close to the wood stove. The wind whistled through the windows, and we did everything we could to stave off the frigid drafts. We bundled up in thick quilts to get relief from shivering.

However, winter provided fun-filled days of bobsledding outside and needlework inside by the fire. I looked out the second story windows to my fairy lane covered with snow, a sparkling sight to my eyes, and thought about the seasons ahead… times when I could be an actress again and roam freely on my stage.

Travelers Share Their Stories

After the evening meal, the collection of strangers sat around the dining table spinning more tales and told stories about adventures experienced on the trail. Our whole family gathered around the circle and listened to the fascinating and colorful stories of the wandering pioneers. One traveler recalled how a man named Carly tired of the trek west and traded a horse for a small piece of land along the

Mississippi. Another man with the last name of Foster told about a family traveling south to Texas to begin a new life. The husband, wife, and three small sons made the journey with their two mules pulling a wagon full of their worldly possessions. When they got to Texas, they found out that swindlers took their money and left no deed for the land. The father sent his family back, first to a sod hut in Nebraska where other

relatives lived, and then back to Iowa. I felt bad when I heard the story and wondered what became of the family. A lady named Colleen, with flaming red hair, told of leaving Ireland for a new life in New York. She heard of opportunities in the West, so she boarded the stagecoach and left on a whim for unknown lands. Some stories made me laugh. One man told of racing his pony against a woman on a bicycle. A little girl bragged about seeing a herd of buffalo along the route and called them "big" cows. Stories of rattlesnakes and water moccasins, difficulty crossing rivers, and so many more added a festive flair to the tales of the rough journey. I loved to listen to the tales strangers spun and wondered if their new lives would be better than mine.

Riding In A Stage

Creeping through the valley, crawling o'er the hill,
Splashing through the branches, rumbling o'er the mill;
Putting nervous gentlemen in a towering rage.
What is so provoking as riding in a stage?

Spinsters fair and forty, maids in youthful charms,
Suddenly are cast into their neighbors' arms;
Children shoot like squirrels darting through a cage–
Isn't it delightful, riding in a stage?

Feet are interlacing, heads severely bumped,
Friend and foe together get their noses thumped;
Dresses act as carpets-listen to the sage;
"Life is but a journey taken in a stage."

By Captain William Banning & George Hugh Banning, 1928

Final Farewells

Everyone rose early in the morning to board the stage. "Hurry up and help with breakfast. The riders need something to eat before leaving," Mama pleaded. She added, "Fill the canteens from the pump, Will." Papa and the farm hand then helped the driver hitch the horses and assisted in placing bags on top of the coach.

I watched as the excited group boarded the stage. I wondered if I would see any of them again. Probably not. The West was a large place, a faraway place, and most would make their home in one of the new towns far from mine.

With a jerk of the reins, the driver yelled, "*Giddy up!*" With a slight lurch, the horses headed down the long dirt path that led to the road. Passengers leaned out the windows and peered for one last look at our stage stop. A long trip lay ahead before another night's rest. They waved and my family waved back. Papa checked his prized pocket watch and knew the coach was leaving on time. "*God speed!*" Papa shouted over the squeaking of the wooden wagon wheels. "*God speed!*"

Hollyhock
"Female Ambition"
Imported to England from China in the Sixteenth Century. The English used the leaves to cure horses' swollen heels.

Many days would pass before another stagecoach came up the dirt path. I dreamed of more stories and new tales. Mama and I climbed the steps to the front porch while Papa and Will went to the barn. A day's work was still ahead.

I hesitated at the front of the porch and leaned out to get one last glance at the stage before it went over the hill. I followed it with my eyes until it dropped out of sight just above the line where the sky and earth met. At that, I wrapped my quilt around my shoulders, turned and twirled to the left and then to the right. For a moment, I was an actress on my imaginary stage again. I gracefully bowed to my audience of prairie grass and wildflowers and looked at the clear blue sky. I nodded to Grandma's colorful red, pink, and white hollyhocks now tall and strong just like me. With a sigh, I turned and walked into the stage stop, my home on the prairie. Now I must wait for the next batch of travelers to come my way.

Seasons came. Seasons went. Years passed. New neighbors arrived. New towns formed. Life constantly changed. But the beloved stage stop and the memories made there remained with me for many years. This was my home, my home on the prairie.

The Chinese consider it the symbol of fruitfulness.
~ The Language of Flowers

What Do You Think?

Would you be afraid to travel by a horse-drawn wagon
with only a few belongings? What would be your fears?
What would you need to bring to survive a long journey?
What would you be willing to leave behind?

How many travelers got discouraged and made
their way back to their old homes?

During Hallie's childhood, animals (horses, oxen, cattle) were used
for transportation. Name a few present time transportation options.
How are they better or worse than the past?

What would you have at a modern day stage stop
that Hallie did not have? List some things that you have
at home that Hallie did not have.

What treasures did Hallie find in the trunk under the staircase?
What treasures would you pack for the trip West?

Spin a tale… imagine you were one of the travelers
and write about your adventure.

How would you design a modern day stagecoach?
Draw a picture of your stagecoach.

Go 3D! Design a stage coach made from a shoe box or similar materials.

Create your own quilt pattern and color with colored pencils.

What would a headline say in a newspaper from the year 1870?
Design a newspaper with headlines and stories from Hallie's day.

About the Author

Rosalie Vandewater Ingle grew up in a house near Orient, Iowa, located within Adair County, that decades before had served as a hotel and stage stop. Ingle's childhood experience in this home was the inspiration for a fictional story portraying life in the Midwest during the Western Expansion of the 1800s. Ingle's love for history and fact finding has given her a true appreciation for the early American pioneers traveling through Iowa along the Mormon Trail heading west. This book brings alive the thoughts and spirit of a young girl as she lives a new life on the Midwestern prairie and gives a glimpse into the "home" that welcomed rugged, adventurous travelers.

Ingle holds a Master's Degree in Education from Northwest Missouri State University. Her career as an English, speech, and drama teacher spanned 27 years. Additionally, her commitment to education continued in writing grants for her school district for four years. Currently Ingle resides in Missouri with her husband. Ingle's two sons and their wives have blessed them with six grandchildren.

Because of an early love for drama and creative writing, Ingle began this journey to capture the spirit of the prairie and lifestyle of a stage stop through a young child's eyes. Her journey continues by sharing her story and the fascinating research of a bygone era through interaction with readers at her blog, www.rosalieinglestagejournal.blogspot.com. Other aspects of her life include collecting antiques, gardening, and traveling.

Author's Note

Hallie is a fictional character, but she represents many young girls who left their first home with their family and found new homes further west on the prairie. Other named characters are also fictional, but they, too, represent the many pioneers of the Western Movement. *The Stage is Coming! Hallie's Stage Stop Journey*, is inspired by an Iowa stage stop. Stagecoach routes crisscrossed Iowa primarily from 1837 to 1874. Short routes ran into the late 70s until railroads took over many, but not all, travel needs. Each stop was different; stops varied in the types of structures and the services offered to travelers, but essentially, they all met the purpose of providing a resting place for weary souls as they made their way to the West. Some travelers rode in stage coaches, while some came in covered wagons or open wagons, and occasionally, on horseback. Research, personal recollections and stories told by others helped in the development of this book.

The stage stop home that inspired this book is located in Adair County, Iowa, outside the small town of Orient. This location is important because it lies directly along the Mormon Trail. I grew up in that very house. My parents lived there before I was born, just like my grandparents and their family did before them; this was a time span of 45 years. My grandfather and my father farmed this land which was owned by Hazel Witham White, the granddaughter of some of the first proprietors of the stage stop. Hazel's grandparents, R. W. and Eliza Johnson bought this land and an already existing roadhouse/stage stop business in the mid 1870s. As a young girl I found Hazel's visits to the farm interesting, and she shared with me many details of life at the roadhouse/stage stop as told by her family members. This treasure of information along with my memories of growing up on the farm and in the house became an integral part of my book, *The Stage is Coming! Hallie's Stage Stop Journey*. The stage stop land is traced back to 1855 when the US government first filed a deed to the original owner. The land changed hands many times before the Johnsons bought it in 1875. From that point on for over one hundred thirty years, it remained in the possession of descendants of the Johnson family. The long running family ownership ended in 2008 when it was sold to a local family. This farm and the farm home served an important role in the development of the West. The wide front porch is gone, but the basic structure of the house, built in the 1870s, still stands just a few yards from a modern Mormon Trail marker.

The name Hallie is derived from the name of my great-grandmother, Mahala. She lived the life of an early pioneer, too.

As a young girl I knew that I lived in a special house. I whirled and twirled on the expansive front porch much like Hallie. I imagined the stage coach rumbling up the dirt road. I pictured travelers staying in the house and reveled in the possible stories they told. I found the rooms and closets fascinating to explore. I sat under trees and roamed the surrounding fields. I wrote my memories down and enlisted the help of others to record what they remembered of this special place. My character, Hallie, brings the story of the stage stop to life.

Photo Left: Rosalie Vandewater, age 1, pictured in front of stage stop home with grandmother Janice Matthews